PRESENTED TO

_____

WITH LOVE FROM

_____

DATE

_____

The kingdom of heaven is of the childlike,
of those who are easy to please,
who love and give pleasure.

ROBERT LOUIS STEVENSON

Illustrations copyright © Thomas Kinkade,
Media Arts Group, Inc., San Jose, CA

Text compilation copyright © 2001 by Tommy Nelson®,
a division of Thomas Nelson, Inc.

Published in Nashville, Tennessee, by Tommy Nelson®,
a division of Thomas Nelson, Inc.

Unless otherwise indicated, Scripture quotations are from the
International Children's Bible®, *New Century Version*®, copyright © 1986, 1988, 1999
by Tommy Nelson®, a division of Thomas Nelson, Inc. Used by permission.

ISBN 0-8499-7769-X

Library of Congress Control Number: 2001132129

Printed in China

01 02 03 04 05 LEO 5 4 3 2 1

THOMAS KINKADE

Classic Prayers

Thomas Nelson, Inc.
Nashville

Our Father in heaven,
we pray that your name will always be kept holy.
We pray that your kingdom will come.
We pray that what you want will be done,
here on earth as it is in heaven.
Give us the food we need for each day.
Forgive the sins we have done,
just as we have forgiven those who did wrong to us.
Do not cause us to be tested;
but save us from the Evil One.

MATTHEW 6:9–13

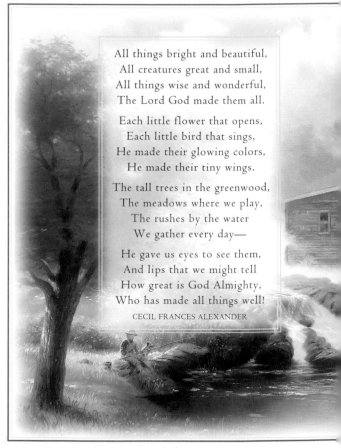

All things bright and beautiful,
All creatures great and small,
All things wise and wonderful,
The Lord God made them all.

Each little flower that opens,
Each little bird that sings,
He made their glowing colors,
He made their tiny wings.

The tall trees in the greenwood,
The meadows where we play,
The rushes by the water
We gather every day—

He gave us eyes to see them,
And lips that we might tell
How great is God Almighty,
Who has made all things well!

CECIL FRANCES ALEXANDER

The LORD is my shepherd;
    I shall not want.
He maketh me to lie down in green pastures:
    he leadeth me beside the still waters.
He restoreth my soul:
    he leadeth me in the paths of righteousness
    for his name's sake.
Yea, though I walk through the valley
    of the shadow of death,
    I will fear no evil;
    for thou art with me;
    thy rod and thy staff they comfort me.
Thou preparest a table before me
    in the presence of mine enemies:
    thou anointest my head with oil;
    my cup runneth over.
Surely goodness and mercy shall follow me
    all the days of my life:
    and I will dwell in the house
    of the LORD for ever.

PSALM 23, KING JAMES VERSION

Dear God,

You are my shepherd.
You give me everything I need.
You give me rest and peace.
You give me new strength,
and you lead me on paths that are right.

Even if I walk through the darkness,
I will not be afraid because I know
that you are always with me.

You prepare a meal for me
in front of my enemies.
You pour oil on my head.
You give me more than I can hold.

I know that your goodness and love
will be with me all my life.
And I will live in the house
of the Lord forever.

[Based on Psalm 23]
TAMA FORTNER

Thank you for my friend next door,
And my friend across the street,
And please help me to be a friend
To everyone I meet.

UNKNOWN

When I wake up in the morning,
    thank you, God, for being there.
When I come to school each day,
    thank you, God, for being there.
When I am playing with my friends,
    thank you, God, for being there.
And when I go to bed at night,
    thank you, God, for being there.

UNKNOWN

Heavenly Father, hear my prayer:
Night and day I'm in Your care;
Look upon me from above,
Bless the home I dearly love;
Bless the friends with whom I play,
Make us kinder day by day.

UNKNOWN

"Love each other.
You must love each other
as I have loved you."

JOHN 13:34

May the love of God our Father
Be in all our homes today:
May the love of the Lord Jesus
Keep our hearts and minds always:
May his loving Holy Spirit
Guide and bless the ones I love,
Father, mother, brothers, sisters,
Keep them safely in his love.

UNKNOWN

Children, obey your parents the way the Lord wants.
This is the right thing to do.

EPHESIANS 6:1–2

Bless, O Lord Jesus, my parents,
And all who love me and take care of me.
Make me loving to them,
Polite and obedient, helpful and kind.
Amen.

UNKNOWN

Bless all parents in their children, and
all children in their parents.

CHRISTINA ROSSETTI

Two little eyes to look to God;

Two little ears to hear his word;

Two little feet to walk in his ways;

Two little lips to sing his praise;

Two little hands to do his will

And one little heart to love him still.

TRADITIONAL from Wales

All for You, dear God.
Everything I do,
Or think,
Or say
The whole day long.
Help me to be good.

UNKNOWN

Lord, teach me all that I should know;
In grace and wisdom I may grow;
The more I learn to do Your will,
The better may I love You still.

ISAAC WATTS (Adapted)

Lord, teach me what you want me to do.

PSALM 86:11

The Lord listens when I pray to him.

PSALM 4:3

Jesus, friend of little children,
  Be a friend to me;
Take my hand and ever keep me
  Close to thee.

Teach me how to grow in goodness
  Daily as I grow:
You have been a child, and surely
  You must know.

Never leave me nor desert me,
  Always be my friend,
I need you from life's beginning
  To its end.

WALTER J. MATHAMS (Adapted)

Be near me, Lord Jesus, I ask Thee to stay,

Close by me forever, and love me, I pray.

Bless all the dear children in Thy tender care,

And take us to heaven, to live with Thee there.

MARTIN LUTHER

God is great, and God is good.
Let us thank Him for our food.
By His hand we all are fed;
Thank you, Lord, for our daily bread.

TRADITIONAL

Our hands we fold,
And heads we bow,
For food and drink
We ask Thee now.
Amen.

UNKNOWN

It is very nice to think
The world is full of meat and drink,
With little children saying grace
In every Christian kind of place.

ROBERT LOUIS STEVENSON

For what we are about to receive,
May the Lord make us truly thankful.
Amen.

TRADITIONAL

Come, Lord Jesus, be our guest,
And may our meal by you be blessed.

MARTIN LUTHER (Adapted)

Lord, teach a little child to pray,
    And then accept my prayer,
    Thou hearest all the words I say
    For Thou art everywhere.

A little sparrow cannot fall
    Unnoticed, Lord, by Thee;
    And though I am so young and small
    Thou dost take care of me.

Teach me to do the thing that's right,
    And when I sin, forgive;
    And make it still my chief delight
    To serve Thee while I live.

JANE TAYLOR

Be near me, Lord Jesus, I ask Thee to stay,
Close by me forever, and love me, I pray.
Bless all the dear children in Thy tender care,
And take us to heaven, to live with Thee there.

MARTIN LUTHER

I can lie down and go to sleep.
And I will wake up again because the Lord protects me.

PSALM 3:5

Now I lay me down to sleep.
I pray You, Lord, my soul to keep.
Your love be with me through the night
And wake me with the morning light.

TRADITIONAL

Lord, You made the stars that brightly
Twinkle in the nighttime sky.
You made the clouds that float lightly
Above the trees and mountains high.
Lord, You know each one by number.
Your watchful eyes never slumber.
O Lord who made the stars above,
Watch me, guard me with Your love.

UNKNOWN

Lord, keep me safe this night,
Secure from all my fears;
May angels guard me while I sleep,
Till morning light appears.

JOHN LELAND (Adapted)

Now before I run to play,
  Let me not forget to pray
To God who kept me through the night
  And waked me with the morning light.
Help me, Lord, love Thee more
  than I ever loved before,
In my work and in my play,
  Be Thou with me through the day.

UNKNOWN

Lord, through this day,
In work and play,
Please bless each thing I do.
May I be honest, loving, kind,
Obedient unto you.

UNKNOWN

The moon shines bright,
The stars give light
Before the break of day;
God bless you all
Both great and small
And send you a joyful day.

TRADITIONAL

Be full of joy in the Lord always.

PHILIPPIANS 4:4

Index of Paintings

4–5	*The Garden of Prayer*
6–7	*The Blessings of Summer*
8–9	*Hidden Arbor*
10	*Hidden Cottage II*
12–13	*Carmel, Ocean Avenue on a Rainy Afternoon*
14	*The Garden of Promise*
16–17	*Bridge of Faith*
18–19	*Village Inn*
20–21	*Hometown Chapel*
22	*Glory of Evening*
25	*Studio in the Garden*
Front cover	*The Mountain Chapel*
Back cover	*Glory of Evening*
Index	*A New Day Dawning*